FANTASTIC YOU

by Danielle Dufayet
illustrated by Jennifer Zivoin

Magination Press • Washington, DC
American Psychological Association

To my grandsons, Christopher
and Roman—may you always know
how fantastic you are!—DD

For my fantastic kids, Olivia and Elyse.—JZ

Books for Kids From the
American Psychological Association

Magination Press is a registered trademark of the American Psychological Association.
Order books at maginationpress.org, or call 1-800-374-2721.

Book design by Sandra Kimbell
Printed by Worzalla, Stevens Point, WI

Library of Congress Cataloging-in-Publication Data
Names: Dufayet, Danielle, author. | Zivoin, Jennifer, illustrator.
Title: Fantastic you / by Danielle Dufayet ; illustrated by Jennifer Zivoin.
Description: Washington, DC : Magination Press, [2019] | "American
Psychological Association." | Summary: Teaches the reader how to develop
and nurture a loving and positive relationship with oneself by engaging in
such behaviors as self-talk and self-compassion throughout the day.
Identifiers: LCCN 2018059305| ISBN 9781433830280 (hardcover) |
ISBN 1433830280 (hardcover)
Subjects: | CYAC: Self-esteem—Fiction. | Self-acceptance—Fiction.
Classification: LCC PZ7.1.D8337 Fan 2019 |
DDC [E]—dc23 LC record available at https://lccn.loc.gov/2018059305

Manufactured in the United States of America
10 9 8 7 6 5 4 3 2 1

There's one special person I'm always with...can you guess who?

So I'm going to give myself the same love and kindness that I give the people I love.

Loving others makes me happy and loving myself does too!

When I wake up, I give myself a smile to start the day off right.

And when I talk (or think) to myself, I choose kind and positive words:

"Hello, awesome!"

If something goes wrong and I say something negative,
like, "I'll never be good enough,"

I stop myself and say something more encouraging:
"It's OK, I just need more practice and patience."

I can cheer myself on: "I can do this!"

And I can cheer myself up, like when I've been waiting all week to go to the beach...

and then I can't.

I cheer myself up by closing
the curtains and putting on a
shadow puppet show,

building a fort,

or giving myself a chocolate
milk mustache.

When cheering myself up doesn't help,
I try not to keep feelings inside.

I talk to someone,

write a letter, poem, or story,

or draw a picture.

I tell my heart: "It's going to be OK."

Sometimes loving me means I stand up for myself. That's when I

roar like a lion,

walk away,

or tell someone.

And when I'm sick or just having a bad day, it's especially important to give myself extra love.

I can snuggle with my softest blanket,

cuddle with my favorite lovey,

or take an extra long, extra bubbly bath.

If I mess up, I say sorry. I do what I can to help make things right, even if it's an accident. Then, I remember to forgive myself.

Instead of feeling bad about what I did, I remind myself:

"Everyone makes mistakes. I'll do better next time."

Just like every person on the planet, I have my unique gifts

and less-than-perfect bits all mixed together.

That's why I'm a work in progress just like everyone else.

This world is amazing and full of ups and downs.

I get to experience it with
all the people I love:

sometimes with my family,

sometimes with my friends...

but, always, with ME!

There's a special person you're going to
be with your whole life. Can you guess who?

Wonderful, awesome,

FANTASTIC

YOU!

Note to Parents and Caregivers

Learning to show yourself love and kindness is an important skill because, as the narrator reflects in *Fantastic You,* the one person you're going to be with your whole life…is you! One way your child can show themselves this love and kindness is by learning to notice, identify, and soothe their own emotions. This important developmental task begins in childhood, but your child will continue to learn about their own emotions, emotional reactions, and how to cope effectively with their feelings throughout their life. As a parent or caretaker, you have ample opportunities to help your child build a strong foundation in this important area.

Identify Emotions

Children are not born with the ability to perfectly identify and label emotions. Instead, young children rely on their environment (i.e., you!) to understand what different surges of emotions and accompanying sensations in their bodies—such as tummy butterflies, tense muscles, and tears—might mean. When you suspect your young child is experiencing a big emotion, get curious with them about what they are feeling. You can ask what is happening inside their body and if they know the name of the emotion they are experiencing. You can also support them in guessing what they feel. For example, you might say "I see that your face is red, and your hands are in fists. When I do those actions, I am often feeling angry. Do you think that's how you are feeling?"

Teach Your Child to Self-Validate

As your child develops the skills of identifying and labeling their emotions, it is also important to teach them that emotions, no matter how big or painful, are safe and acceptable to experience. The best way to teach this important lesson is to validate their emotions—to communicate that you see their emotions and that they make sense. Parents do this regularly, for example saying, "I see that you are really angry right now," or "given that it is raining, and you can't go to the beach, it makes sense that you would feel sad." However, it is also important for children to learn how to "self-validate" or to reassure themselves that their emotions are acceptable and not something to be ashamed of. This is an important skill because when a child validates themselves, it can bring down the intensity of an emotion in the moment. It also helps to build healthy respect for and trust in their ability to manage their own feelings.

Children (and adults!) often have the urge to avoid or deny uncomfortable emotions, such as anger and shame. However, by paying attention to and validating these painful feelings, such as by saying

"I'm feeling angry right now and that's okay," or "I feel embarrassed that I was not a kind friend," a child sets themselves up to make more effective and self-respecting choices. When the child in the story accepts that she is angry and needs to stand up for herself, she then has a range of positive choices in front of her, including walking away or asking an adult for help. Similarly, by acknowledging embarrassment or shame over "messing up," the child is able to apologize and to forgive herself. In contrast, if a child invalidates, or tells themselves that their feelings are stupid or don't make sense, they tend to become more upset and to make poor choices such as lashing out in anger or blaming others.

Self-Soothe When Upset

Help your child discover which activities or experiences soothe them when they are upset. There are unlimited ways to "self-soothe" and it takes trial and error for a child to develop their own "user manual" and figure out what works best for them. For most children, the ideal self-soothing activity depends on the situation as well as their own preferences. Some children enjoy calming themselves by soothing their senses, for example by taking extra-long, extra bubbly baths, listening to calming music, stretching, or watching the clouds. Other children find distraction and play like building forts or putting on a puppet show to be most helpful. Take a fun, creative approach in helping your child try out many different activities to calm their strong emotions. Though it can often feel like play, learning to self-soothe is a critical skill your child will use throughout their life.

Teach Helpful Self-Talk

Teach your child to say kind, positive, and encouraging comments to themselves, as the children in the book learn to do. Help your child notice the power of their own "self-talk," or what they say to themselves in tough moments. When a child puts themselves down—for example, telling themselves "I'll never be good enough" when they struggle with basketball—they usually feel even worse. When they feel worse, they are more likely to act in ways that they will not feel proud of later, such as quitting or avoiding the difficult activity or having a tantrum.

Once your child understands how powerful and important their self-talk is, help them develop and practice more helpful phrases they might say to themselves during difficult moments. It can be helpful for children to rehearse a few go-to encouraging phrases, such as "this is hard, but I can do it if I keep trying" and "I feel frustrated, but I know I can stay cool." Practicing this skill in calm moments can help children use encouraging and positive language during challenges.

Model Constructive Coping and Self-Care

Parents can experience tremendous societal and internal pressure to put their children's needs above their own; however, one of your most important jobs as a parent is to teach your children the importance of loving and caring for oneself. When you are feeling upset about something that is appropriate for your child to hear about, consider labeling the emotion and sharing with your child how you plan to cope with it. For example, you might say "I feel sad that I had a hard day at work. To take care of myself and my feelings, I'm going to go for a long walk with the dog and take a bath later tonight."

When to Seek Support

Developing the ability to cope with powerful emotions is an important developmental task that children master at different times. Additionally, it is typical for developing children and teens to go through phases in which they cope more and less skillfully with powerful emotions (just think of the terrible twos and adolescence!).

However, if your child consistently has trouble coping with their painful emotions—getting stuck in negative, self-critical thoughts, taking a very long time to recover after disappointments, showing intense, prolonged shame after making mistakes, or consistently struggling to apologize when appropriate—consider seeking professional support. Consult with a licensed psychologist or other mental health professional who specializes in cognitive behavioral therapy (CBT) for children.

Julia Martin Burch, PhD, is a staff psychologist at the McLean Anxiety Mastery Program at McLean Hospital in Boston. Dr. Martin Burch completed her training at Fairleigh Dickinson University and Massachusetts General Hospital/Harvard Medical School. She works with children, teens, and parents, and specializes in cognitive behavioral therapy for anxiety, obsessive compulsive, and related disorders.

About the Author

Danielle Dufayet is an author who also teaches English and public speaking/self-empowerment classes for kids. She has a bachelor's in English literature and a master's in psychology. She has always been drawn to the beauty and simplicity of picture books and attracted by their powerful psychological impact on young minds. She believes that books are magic little gems that can change one's life. She lives in San Jose, California. Visit danielledufayetbooks.com.

About the Illustrator

Jennifer Zivoin is trained in media ranging from figure drawing to virtual reality and earned her bachelor of arts degree with highest distinction from the honors division of Indiana University. Jennifer worked as a graphic designer and creative director before finding her artistic niche in children's books. She has illustrated more than 30 books, including *You Are Your Strong, Something Happened in Our Town: A Child's Story About Racial Injustice,* and *A World of Pausabilities: An Exercise in Mindfulness.* Jennifer lives in Carmel, Indiana. Visit JZArtworks.com.

About Magination Press

Magination Press is the children's book imprint of the American Psychological Association. Through APA's publications, the association shares with the world mental health expertise and psychological knowledge. Magination Press books reach young readers and their parents and caregivers to make navigating life's challenges a little easier. It's the combined power of psychology and literature that makes a Magination Press book special. Visit maginationpress.org.